LET'S HAVE A PARTY #3

SLEEPOVER

LET'S HAVE A PARTY #3

SLEEPOVER

LAURA E. WILLIAMS

Illustrations by George Ulrich

AN AVON CAMELOT BOOK

AVON BOOKS
A division of
The Hearst Corporation
1350 Avenue of the Americas
New York, New York 10019

Copyright © 1997 by Laura E. Williams
Interior illustrations copyright © 1997 by Avon Books
Interior illustrations by George Ulrich
Published by arrangement with the author
Visit our website at **http://AvonBooks.com**
Library of Congress Catalog Card Number: 97-92889
ISBN: 0-380-78924-8
RL: 2.3

First Avon Camelot Printing: August 1997

CAMELOT TRADEMARK REG. U.S. PAT. OFF. AND IN OTHER COUNTRIES, MARCA REGISTRADA, HECHO EN U.S.A.

Printed in the U.S.A.

OPM   10 9 8 7 6 5 4 3 2 1

*This book is dedicated to
the supportive students, teachers, and staff of
the Manchester, CT, school system—
for listening patiently to all my ideas and
even brainstorming a few with me, and
for not rolling your eyes whenever I said,
"Hey, I've got another idea! Want to hear it?"*

1

Tonight!

Tasha Kearney painted the last petal on the flower.

Molly leaned over the painting. "That is soooo good," she said with a sigh. "You are the best artist I know."

Tasha dipped her paintbrush in the water glass. "Thanks," she said with a big smile. "I'm going to give it to my mom for letting me have a sleepover party."

"I can't wait until tonight. What are we going to do?" Pegi asked, closing the jar of green paint.

"Eat a lot of food, build a tent, and tell scary stories. The rest will have to be a surprise," Tasha said.

"I know a great story to tell at your party," Maryellen said. "It's really, really scary."

Ricky walked by with his arms full of paint jars. He stopped next to the table. "Is tonight the big party?"

Tasha grinned. "That's right. Tonight is my sleepover party."

"But you're not invited," Molly said with a smile. "Only girls are allowed."

Ricky shrugged. "That's okay. We guys are going over to Timmy's house. We're going to do cool things. Cooler than anything girls can do."

"Like what?" Tasha asked.

Ricky's face turned red. "Uh, like . . . Uh, I have to put these paints away." He hurried away.

The girls laughed.

"Poor Ricky," Pegi said. "When will he learn that girls can do anything boys can do?"

"And do it even better!" Lesley added, looking up from her painting of a horse.

That made everyone laugh harder.

Pretty soon the camp counselor clapped his hands. "Time to clean up," he said. "It's almost time to go home."

Tasha and her friends rushed around cleaning up. Paintings were hung on the board to dry. Paint spills were wiped up. Brushes were washed with soap and water.

Finally it was time to go home.

"See you later," Tasha said, waving to her friends.

"Have a good time tonight," Jamal said, jumping onto his bike.

"Yeah," Timmy added. "Don't let the boogeyman get you girls." He hooted with laughter.

Oliver rolled his eyes. "Don't pay attention to him," he said politely. "He's just being silly."

Tasha smiled. "I never pay attention to him. And he's *always* being silly."

Tasha quickly walked down Lemon Lime

Drive. Her house was only three minutes away from the recreation center at Huckleberry Park.

At home, she burst through the front door. "I'm home!" she called.

No one answered her.

She ran upstairs, looking for her mother. Her mother's room was empty. She was probably in the basement with her rock sculptures.

She noticed Tyrone's bedroom door was shut. He was always up to trouble when his door was shut. Tasha pressed her ear to the door. She could hear him talking to someone.

"That will scare the socks off those little kids," Ty said.

Tasha scowled. He always called her a little kid. She listened more closely.

"And we'll make scary howling noises."

Ty was silent for a moment. Then he burst out laughing. "I can't wait until tonight," he said between laughs. "Come over early so we can plan it."

Tasha stomped down the stairs.

She had overheard her rotten brother's plans. He wanted to ruin her birthday party!

But why? What had she ever done to him?

She had already apologized for popping his basketball with the screwdriver. And she hadn't meant to run over his plastic car with her bike. And she had cleaned up the paint off his carpet.

So why did he want to ruin her sleepover party?

Tasha shook her head. It didn't matter. Now that she knew his plans, he *couldn't* ruin her party.

She grinned. No matter what those boys tried to do, they wouldn't scare her. *Nothing* would ruin her sleepover party!

2

An Unexpected Guest

Later that afternoon, Tasha twirled in the middle of the floor. "Eight is great!" she said out loud.

"What, honey?" called her mother from the kitchen.

"Nothing, Mom," Tasha called back. "I just said eight is great!"

Mrs. Kearney came into the living room. "It sure is. Our fizzy drinks and the party mix are ready to go."

"Mom, you mean the Funtastic Fizzle and the Good Golly Gobs."

"Sorry. Next time, I'll remember to call them by the right names."

"My friends will be here any minute," Tasha said, jumping up and down.

Just then the doorbell rang.

Tasha dashed to the door. She flung it open. Her uncle and his dog stood on the front step.

"Happy Birthday," Uncle Craig said.

"Thanks," Tasha said.

"You don't look very excited," he said.

Tasha smiled. "I'm excited. It's just that I thought you were my first guest. But you're only Uncle Craig."

Uncle Craig put a hand over his heart. He staggered back a step. "Only?"

Tasha laughed. She hugged her uncle. "You know what I mean."

Just then the dog barked. Uncle Craig pulled on the leash. "And don't forget Daffy," he said.

Tasha giggled. "I could never forget Daffy, the tailless wonder." She scratched behind Daffy's ears.

"Old English sheepdogs aren't supposed to have tails," Uncle Craig explained.

"I know," Tasha said with a giggle. "But I still think she looks funny with no tail to wag."

"Craig, what are you doing here?" Mrs. Kearney asked.

He held out Daffy's leash. "Uh, I was hoping you would dog-sit for me," said Uncle Craig. He smiled hopefully. "I'm going on a fishing trip for the weekend. No dogs allowed."

"You should have called first," Mrs. Kearney said.

"But you usually don't mind," Uncle Craig said. "And Daffy loves to stay with you."

"But Tasha is having a slumber party tonight," Mrs. Kearney protested.

Uncle Craig's face fell. His shoulders drooped. "Then what will I do with her? I can't take her fishing. She'll scare all the fish away like she did last time."

"I don't mind," Tasha said quickly. "Daffy can be one of my guests." She took the leash from her uncle. "Daffy can protect us tonight. We're sleeping outside on the porch."

Uncle Craig chuckled. "I wouldn't count on Daffy protecting you. She's a scaredy-cat."

"You mean a scaredy-dog," Tasha said.

At that moment the phone rang. With a "woof," Daffy bolted. Tasha had to let go of the leash. Daffy hid behind the couch. Her gray-and-white fur shook as she trembled with fear.

Tasha and her mother laughed.

Uncle Craig rolled his eyes. "See what I mean?"

3

They're Here!

Uncle Craig left, and Tasha patted Daffy until the dog stopped trembling. When the doorbell rang, Tasha jumped up. She threw it open.

"Happy birthday!" Maryellen said. She handed Tasha a gift. The wrapping paper had cats on it. Maryellen loved cats.

Tasha grinned. "Thank you. Come on in. You're the only one here."

But not for long. Pretty soon the doorbell rang again.

This time Lesley and Lucy arrived together.

"Where should we put our sleeping bags?" Lesley asked. She held up a bag covered with horseshoes.

"Put them on the porch. We'll sleep out there," Tasha said. "And the presents go in here." She pointed to the living room.

"We're going to sleep outside?" Lucy asked. She shivered. "Won't it be scary?"

Tasha shook her head. "We have Daffy to protect us."

Daffy yipped and panted. She tried to wag her tail. But it didn't work because she didn't have a tail. Instead, Daffy's whole rear end wiggled back and forth like a tubful of Jell-O.

The girls laughed.

The doorbell rang again. This time, Ty ran to the door.

"Hi, Ty," said his friend Chad.

"Hi," Ty said. "I saw you coming from my window."

The two boys grinned at each other.

Chad handed something to Ty.

Tasha tried to see what it was. But Ty hid it behind his back.

"Hi, Chad," Tasha said.

"Hi," Chad said. "I heard today is your birthday."

"That's right," Tasha said.

Chad grinned. "I thought so. A little snake told me."

Ty dug his elbow into Chad's ribs.

Tasha saw the way her brother and Chad were trying not to laugh. "What's so funny?" she asked suspiciously.

"Oh, nothing," Ty said quickly. "Come on, Chad, let's go upstairs."

The boys raced out of the room.

Tasha could hear them laugh all the way up the stairs. Then she heard Ty's door slam shut.

Let them laugh, she thought. Whatever they were planning, it wouldn't scare her!

Next time the doorbell rang, Pegi was standing there. Pegi's father Mr. Parmetti honked the horn as he drove away.

Tasha waved.

"Happy birthday," Pegi said, tugging on her

baseball cap. "I had my dad drive me because I was late. Am I the last one here?"

Tasha shook her head. "We're still waiting for Molly and Judy."

"Good," Pegi said. "I hate being the last one to a party. Here's your present."

Tasha took the big gift and shook it. Something thunked inside. "Thank you," she said. "I can't wait to open it."

Pegi smiled. "I think you'll like it. I almost wanted to keep it for myself."

Before Tasha could close the door, Judy and Molly ran up the front walkway.

"Sorry we're late," Judy said out of breath. "I had to feed my baby squirrel."

"I'm late because I watched her," Molly said. "The squirrel is *so* cute."

"That's okay," Tasha said. She knew Judy would do anything to save an injured or lost animal. "I'm glad you're here now."

"So are we," Judy and Molly said together. Molly handed Tasha a present.

Judy noticed Daffy hiding behind Tasha's legs and said, "I didn't know you had a dog!"

"Daffy is my uncle's dog. Tonight he's a guest at my party," Tasha said.

"I love dogs," Judy said as she handed Tasha a present and got on her knees to play with Daffy.

Tasha beamed. One great thing about birthdays was the presents. But even better than that was having all her friends over for a sleepover party!

4

The Mysterious Present

"**O**pen your presents," Lesley cried. "I hope you like what I got for you."

Pegi patted Tasha on the back. "I *know* you'll like my gift."

Tasha grinned. "I like *all* presents!"

Mrs. Kearney ushered the girls into the living room. "Don't open your presents yet," she said. "Wait while I get your snacks and my camera."

Tasha looked at the bright packages. They looked wonderful. She couldn't wait to open them.

It seemed as if a year went by. Finally, Tasha's mother came back with tall, fancy drinks and a big bowl full of something.

"What pretty drinks," Lucy said.

Tasha handed her a glass. "I call it a Funtastic Fizzle."

Lucy took a sip and then giggled. "It fizzles in your mouth!"

"And what's this?" Judy asked, peering into the bowl. "It looks like something I'd feed one of my stray animals."

Maryellen laughed. "I hope it tastes better than that."

"It looks like trail mix I take on my hiking trips," Molly said.

Tasha passed around the bowl. "I call it Good Golly Gobs."

"Mmmm, yummy," Lesley said, reaching for more.

Tasha licked her fingers. "Did you get your camera?" she asked her mother.

Mrs. Kearney pulled the camera out of her

pocket. "I sure did. Now you may open your presents."

"Yippee!" Tasha carefully pulled on the pink ribbon around her first gift.

Her friends watched with wide eyes. They all smiled.

Lesley giggled. "That one's from me."

"I can tell," Tasha said. "I love the pony you drew on the wrapping paper. It looks just like your pony Lightning."

Finally the ribbon came off. Next, Tasha slowly pulled at the tape.

Maryellen sighed. "Can't you just rip off the paper?"

"Yeah, rip it off," said all the girls.

Tasha hesitated for only one second. Then she laughed and ripped the wrapping paper. But she was careful not to rip Lesley's drawing.

"Oooo," she said. She held up the package of glitter pens and colorful paper. "I love it. Thank you."

Lesley beamed. "I picked it out just for you because you love to draw."

"Now open mine," Pegi said. "It's the one with the baseballs and bats on the paper."

Before Tasha knew it, almost all her presents were open. There was only one left.

She held up the gift. It was wrapped in wrinkled green paper. "Who is this from?" she asked.

Her friends looked at each other. Then they looked back at her. They shrugged.

"Not me," Lucy said. "I gave you the doll."

"I gave you the pink racing car," Maryellen said.

"I gave you the stuffed bunny," Judy said.

"And I gave you the private-eye set," Molly said.

Tasha turned to her mother. "Then who is it from?"

Mrs. Kearney looked confused too. "I don't know. Why don't you just open it. Maybe there's a card inside."

Tasha unwrapped the package. Inside was an old shoe box.

"What's in it?" Pegi asked. She leaned forward, trying to see.

Tasha lifted the lid. "Eeeek," she shrieked. She threw the box in the air.

5

Brother Trouble

When the box landed on the floor, a snake slithered out!

The girls squealed and lifted their feet. Lucy squealed louder than the rest.

Tasha stared at the slimy green snake. "Hey," she said after a minute, "it's not moving."

"Is it dead?" Lucy asked between squeals.

Tasha nudged the snake with her shoe. Then

she picked it up. She swung it over her head and held it in the air. "It's made of rubber!"

Just then, Ty and Chad fell into the room. They were laughing so hard, tears filled their eyes.

"That was a stupid joke," Tasha yelled. "It wasn't even funny."

The boys couldn't stop laughing.

"Mom, tell them to stop!"

Mrs. Kearney leaned over the boys. They were still on the floor laughing.

"Boys, that was not very nice. Behave yourselves or you won't be allowed out of Ty's room."

Ty and Chad finally stood up. Ty turned to his friend. "Did you see the way she threw the box in the air?"

Chad nodded. "Did you hear them scream?"

Still laughing, the boys scrambled back upstairs.

Tasha glared after them. They would not scare her again. Not even if they gave her *one hundred* rubber snakes!

Lesley put her hand over her mouth. A giggle escaped anyway.

Tasha crossed her arms. "What are you laughing at?" she demanded.

"Well, you did look kind of funny," Lesley admitted.

Judy smiled. "And did you hear Lucy squeal?"

Lucy giggled. "My mother tells me I sound like a baby pig when I squeal like that."

Tasha laughed. She couldn't help it. "I guess it was pretty funny. But don't tell the boys. They'll just plan more tricks."

Tasha looked around the room. "Hey, where's Daffy?"

Just then a whimper came from behind the couch.

"Here she is," Mrs. Kearney said. "Your brave watchdog is afraid of snakes."

"Even rubber ones," Tasha said, laughing.

Mrs. Kearney left the room.

Tasha brought out a bag from under the coffee table.

"What's that?" Pegi asked. "More snakes?"

Tasha groaned. "Would I do that to my friends?" She pulled out a tray of paints and several brushes. "This is special face paint."

"Cool," Molly said. "Can you paint a snake

on my cheek? That way I'll really remember this party."

Everyone laughed.

Tasha painted the snake, then she painted a unicorn and a rainbow on Lucy's cheek.

"I want a baseball glove, ball, and bat," Pegi said. "You know it's my favorite sport."

"And I want a puppy with big, sad eyes," Judy said. "Just like the one I saved from the dog pound last month."

Finally, only Tasha's cheek needed painting. "Who wants to paint my cheek?" she asked.

"I'll just mess it up," Molly said, backing away.

"You're the best artist," Lucy said to Tasha. "You'll have to paint your own face."

So Tasha stood in front of a mirror and painted a smiling sun on her cheek.

Just then, Mrs. Kearney poked her head around the kitchen door. "Is anyone hungry?"

6

Making Pizza

All the girls cheered.

Mrs. Kearney smiled. "Then I think it's time to make the pizzas!"

Lucy gasped. "Are we going to make pizzas ourselves?"

Tasha nodded and grinned. "We have all different kinds of toppings."

"We always buy our pizzas," Pegi said. "We have to buy four to feed all my brothers."

Tasha led her friends into the kitchen. "Making them is more fun. Come on."

"First, you all must wash your hands," Mrs. Kearney instructed.

When they finished, the girls lined up at the counter.

Mrs. Kearney put two pans in front of them and one off to the side. Each pan had a lump of dough on it. "Spread the dough. Then you can put your toppings on it."

"Who's the third pizza for?" Tasha asked.

Ty and Chad walked into the kitchen. "For us," Ty said.

Tasha groaned.

"Now remember," Mrs. Kearney said to the boys, "you promised to behave yourselves. If you don't, you will have to stay in Ty's room."

Ty laughed. "Don't worry, Mom. We'll be good. Right, Chad?"

Chad laughed and nodded. "We're always good. Aren't we, Mrs. Kearney?"

Mrs. Kearney lifted one eyebrow. She didn't say yes or no.

Tasha frowned. She did not trust those boys for one second.

"Ewwww." Lucy squealed like a pig again. "The dough is warm and squishy."

Judy giggled. "This is fun." She spread the dough out flat on the pan.

Next they spread tomato sauce on the dough.

"Ooops," Molly said. She looked down at the red sauce she had spilled on the floor.

Pegi rushed to get a wet paper towel. She mopped up the mess.

"Thank you, Pegi," Mrs. Kearney said.

"No problem," Pegi said. "I'm used to cleaning up after my five sloppy brothers."

"Now we're ready for the toppings," Tasha said.

Mrs. Kearney brought out a tray of goodies.

"Yum," Maryellen said. "Olives are my favorite. But keep the onions away from me."

"And we have to have mushrooms. That's my all-time favorite vegetable," Judy added. She picked out the biggest slices.

"I like green peppers and pineapple," Tasha said. She scooped some onto her section of the pizza.

Ty opened the refrigerator. "I like pickles on my pizza. How about you, Chad?"

Chad nodded. "And don't forget the sliced hotdogs."

"And lots and lots of spicy onions," Ty added.

"Yuck," Tasha said. "You boys are gross."

"Don't forget," said Mrs. Kearney, "whatever you boys make, you have to eat."

"Don't worry, Mom," Ty said, grinning.

The girls spread cheese over their pizzas.

The boys spread peanut butter over theirs.

Mrs. Kearney put on an oven glove. "Now I'll cook the pizzas. I'll call you when they're done."

Ty rubbed his hands together. "I can't wait to eat our pizza."

"It sure does look good," Chad said.

"You mean, it looks stupid," Tasha corrected.

"Not as stupid as you looked when you saw the snake!" Ty said.

Tasha squinted her eyes and ground her teeth together. Just ignore them, she told herself. No matter what, she could not let them ruin her birthday party.

7

Noises In The Kitchen

"Let's set up the tents," Tasha said. "The pizzas won't take too long to cook."

The girls marched onto the porch.

The boys followed them. They scratched under their arms like monkeys and said, "Oo, oo, oo."

Tasha glared at them. "Oo, oo, oo to you too."

Her friends giggled.

Tasha grabbed a sheet. "Go away, you two. Mom said you're not allowed to bother us."

The boys left, still acting like monkeys.

"My brother thinks he's funny."

Maryellen sighed. "I think he's cute."

Tasha rolled her eyes. "Cute? He acts like a monkey and looks like one too."

"Come on," Pegi said. "Show us how to set up the tents."

"It's a good thing it's such a warm night," Molly said.

Tasha moved chairs. Then she draped a sheet over them. She crawled under the sheet.

Maryellen joined her. "Hey, this is neat."

Judy popped her head into the tent. "But it isn't big enough for all of us."

"No problem," Tasha said. "We'll make it bigger."

The girls rearranged two more patio chairs to make a big circle.

"My family goes camping every year," Molly said. "This summer we went to Yellowstone."

"I know," Tasha said, pulling one of the chairs into position. "You sent us all postcards."

Maryellen giggled. "And you told me about how you almost got eaten by a bear."

"The poor bear," Judy said with a laugh.

When the chairs were in order, the girls draped the sheet over them.

"Look at that gap," Molly said. "We need something to cover it."

Tasha dashed into the house. She came back carrying a bright pink sheet. "Mom says the pizzas are done. Now they just have to cool for a few minutes."

"Goody," Pegi said. "I'm starving."

Tasha handed Lucy the sheet. "You're taller than the rest of us. Can you reach the gap?"

Lucy flapped open the sheet. Then she used it to cover the hole in the tent.

"Perfect," Tasha exclaimed.

The girls stood back and looked at their creation.

"It looks as crooked as that cat's tail I saved last week," Judy said, tipping her head to one side.

"Let's see what it looks like from the inside," Pegi suggested.

Carefully, the girls slipped under the sheets.

"Cool."

"Awesome."

"Look how that pink sheet glows."

Judy giggled. "It looks like a giant piece of bubblegum."

"And I'm so hungry I could eat the whole piece," Molly said.

"Maybe the pizzas are cooled," Tasha said.

Just then they heard a strange snorting and snuffling.

"What is that?" Lucy whispered.

Tasha's eyes opened wide. "I don't know," she whispered back.

"It's coming from inside the house."

Suddenly Mrs. Kearney shrieked, "Oh no!"

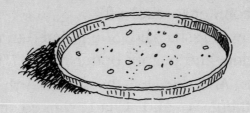

8

Disaster

Tasha and her friends ran into the kitchen.

Tasha got there first. "What is it, Mom?"

Mrs. Kearney pointed to the pizza pans. "Just look at that."

"Oh no," all the girls cried.

Two of the pizzas were gone. Not a crumb left.

"Who ate them?" Lesley asked.

Mrs. Kearney shook her head. "I don't know what could have happened to them. I put them on the counter to cool off."

"I know," Tasha said. She pointed to the hot-dog, pickle, and peanut butter pizza. "The boys ate them. And they left theirs for later."

Just then Ty and Chad walked into the kitchen.

"What's going on?" Ty asked.

"As if you didn't know!" Tasha yelled at them. "You're trying to ruin my party."

Ty's mouth dropped open. "What are you talking about?"

"Ty," said Mrs. Kearney, "did you boys eat these pizzas?"

"No way, Mom," Ty protested.

Tasha glared at her brother. "Well they didn't just disappear all by themselves. You must have eaten them!"

Ty scowled. "We did not!"

"Then who did?" Tasha demanded. "A ghost?"

Ty held his hands up and waved them like a ghost. "That's right. Ooooooo," he howled. "I waaaant your piiiizzaaaaa."

Mrs. Kearney rubbed her forehead. "That's enough. Boys, you just stay out of the way from now on."

"But, Mom—"

Mrs. Kearney held up her hand for silence. "I'll order a pizza from the Pizza Stop. You boys will eat in the kitchen. The girls will eat in the dining room."

Tasha's mother turned and picked up the phone.

Ty stuck his tongue out at Tasha.

Tasha shook her head. Her brother was older than she was, but he sure acted like a baby. She waved her friends into the living room.

"I just know my brother is guilty," she whispered.

"How can we prove it?" Pegi asked.

Molly picked up the present she had given Tasha. "We can use this."

"Perfect!" Tasha exclaimed. She took the private-eye set and opened it. She grabbed the magnifiying glass. "All we have to do is follow the trail of crumbs up to Ty's room."

The girls rushed back into the kitchen.

Tasha examined the floor with the magnifying glass.

"Well? What do you see?" Pegi demanded.

Tasha shook her head. "I don't understand. I don't see hardly *any* crumbs at all!"

Pegi took the magnifying glass. She inspected the floor and then the counter. "She's right," she said to the other girls. "The only crumbs are on the counter. There is no trail."

Tasha led everyone back into the living room. She took out the Super Duper Spying Snooper. "What's this? It looks like a doctor's stethoscope."

Molly showed her how it worked. "It's to listen at doors and through walls."

Tasha's eyes lit up. "Maybe we can catch Ty and Chad talking about their crime."

The girls tiptoed up the stairs. Trying not to giggle, they stood next to Ty's bedroom door.

Carefully, Tasha placed the cone end of the Super Duper Spying Snooper against the door. She put the other end in her ears. She listened silently for a few minutes while Pegi searched the floor for crumbs.

Finally she pulled away from the door.

"It's no use," she said. "They're just talking about dumb stuff like video games and baseball teams."

"Hey," Pegi said. "Baseball teams are not dumb."

Tasha grinned. "They were talking about the Boston Red Sox."

Pegi held her neck and made choking sounds. "Argh," she cried. "Don't they know that the New York Yankees are the *only* team worth talking about?"

Tasha laughed. "We'd better go downstairs before the boys hear us."

Just then, the doorbell rang. Mrs. Kearney opened the door.

"Pizza Stop delivery," a voice said.

"Yeah!" the girls cheered.

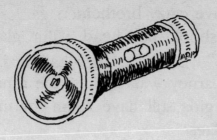

9

Ghost Story

Maryellen sat back with a sigh. "That was great pizza. I'm stuffed."

Tasha wiped pizza sauce off her chin. "Not as good as homemade, though."

"I can't believe your brother ate our pizzas," Judy said, shaking her head. Her short, black hair swished against her cheeks.

"I can," Pegi said. "I know what older brothers can be like. You think you have it bad. Imagine five crazy brothers."

Tasha shook her head. "I'm glad I only have one."

Mrs. Kearney walked into the dining room. "Do you girls still have room for make-your-own sundaes?"

"More food?" Maryellen groaned. Then she smiled. "Okay!"

Her friends laughed.

They piled their sundaes high with nuts and chocolate sauce and bananas and whipped cream.

Molly stared at Maryellen's huge sundae. "I thought you were stuffed," she said.

Maryellen shrugged. "I'm never too stuffed for dessert!"

"Me neither," Mrs. Kearney agreed with a laugh.

When they were finished eating, Tasha pushed away from the table. "Oooo, my aching tummy. I think I ate too much."

"I did too," Lesley said.

"Let's go in the tent now," Tasha suggested. "We can play light as a feather."

"What's that?" Judy asked.

Tasha explained. "One person lies down in the middle. Everyone else puts two fingers under her. Then someone makes up a story about that person and she becomes light as a feather and stiff as a board. And on the count of three everyone lifts up the person in the middle."

"That's sounds scary," Lucy said with a shiver.

Judy frowned. "But how do we lift the middle person with just two fingers?"

Tasha shrugged. "It only works if everyone gets in a trance. Then the middle person really is as light as a feather and stiff as a board."

"Don't scare yourselves too much," Mrs. Kearney said with a smile.

"Just don't let the boys bother us," Tasha said.

Mrs. Kearney patted her head. "Your father is going to watch a movie with them when he gets home. He'll make sure they stay away from you."

Tasha beamed. "Thanks, Mom."

The girls followed Tasha onto the patio and into their tent.

"It's pretty dark in here," Lucy said.

"All the better for our scary stories," Pegi said.

Tasha spread out her sleeping bag. Her friends did the same.

"Who wants to be in the middle first?" she asked.

Lucy raised her hand. "I will. I want to get this over with."

Tasha laughed. "Don't worry, it's not really that scary. It's just fun."

Lucy lay down and crossed her arms over her chest. The rest of the girls lined up on either side of her. They all placed two fingers under her.

When they were settled, Tasha looked around the tent. "Now who wants to tell the first story?"

"I will," Maryellen said.

"Don't make it too scary," Lucy begged, struggling to sit up.

Judy gave a monster chuckle and gently

pushed Lucy back down. "You mean, the scarier the better!"

Lucy squealed.

"Here," said Tasha. "You can hold my hand if you get scared."

Lucy smiled. "Thanks, Tasha."

Maryellen stared down at Lucy. "Close your eyes."

Lucy half closed her eyes.

"All the way," Tasha ordered.

With a sigh, Lucy did as she was told.

Maryellen leaned forward. She lowered her voice. "It happened long ago. On a dark, dark night, in the middle of a cemetery—"

"Oh!" Lucy cried, her eyes popping open. "It's scary already."

Tasha took her friend's arm and squeezed it. "Shhh, let her tell the story. Now close your eyes."

Maryellen continued. "In the cemetery, in the darkest corner—"

"What was that?" Lucy whispered. She kept her eyes squished closed. "I heard something right outside the tent."

10

Noises In The Dark

The girls sat silently and listened.

"I don't hear anything," Pegi finally said.

Judy patted one of Lucy's crossed arms. "It must just be your imagination."

"That's right," said Maryellen. "You just *thought* you heard something."

"Or maybe it was just the wind," Lesley suggested.

The girls listened a few more minutes. No sound came from outside.

Lucy slowly opened her eyes and peered up at them. She grinned sheepishly. "You must be right. It was only the wind. I promise I won't stop the story again." She closed her eyes.

Maryellen continued with the story. "In the deepest, darkest corner of the cemetery, there was an old tombstone with the name Samantha carved on it. Under her name were the years 1836—1846.

"One windy night, Lucy had to walk through the cemetery to get home. As she walked by Samantha's grave, she heard a soft voice say, 'Help meeeeeee, help meeeeeee. Pleeeeease, heeeeelp meeeeeee.' "

Maryellen took a deep breath. "Lucy was so scared, she couldn't move. Her hair stood up on the back of her neck. A shiver shook her knees.

"In the dark night, Lucy thought she saw bony fingers coming toward her. Bony like a skeleton.

"The fingers reached out. Something cold

touched Lucy's cheek. She screamed, and she felt her heart stop. She—"

Suddenly, a loud gurgling sound filled the tent.

Lucy squealed. She bolted up into a sitting position. "There it is again! I knew I heard something before!"

Lesley nodded. "And I don't think that was the wind!"

"It must be a monster," Judy whispered. She pulled her animal sleeping bag over her head.

"Or a ghost," said Molly. Her hands trembled with fear.

"It sounded like a werewolf to me," Maryellen said. "Maybe he's hungry!"

Lucy squealed again.

Tasha began to laugh. She laughed so hard she had to hold her belly.

"Shhh," hissed Molly.

"You snort like my pony when you laugh so hard," Lesley said in a whisper.

Tasha tried to stop laughing, but it was no use.

"What's so funny?" Lucy demanded.

Tasha tried to talk. "Sor—sorry," she gasped.

The strange noise suddenly got closer to the tent. There was also a sharp click, click, click sound.

The girls huddled together. All except Tasha.

Finally she stopped laughing. "It's nothing to be afraid of. It's only my stupid brother and Chad. They're trying to scare us."

"Are you sure?" Lucy asked. She still looked frightened.

Tasha nodded. "I'm sure. I'll be right back."

She crawled out of the tent. She looked around. The boys were nowhere in sight.

Walking across the porch, she peeked in the window. Suddenly she froze. No, it couldn't be!

11

Safe Inside?

For a moment, Tasha couldn't move. Her bare feet stuck to the patio like wet pancake batter.

She blinked her eyes. Was she seeing things?

No, there were Ty and Chad in the living room. They were sprawled on the couch with Dad. The television was on.

If they were *inside* with Dad, where were the noises *outside* coming from?

"Oh no!" Tasha cried. She scrambled back into the tent.

"What's wrong?" Pegi asked.

"We have to go inside. Quick!" Tasha yelled. "The noises weren't Ty and Chad."

"Then what were they?" Lucy cried.

Tasha grabbed her sleeping bag. "I don't know," she wailed.

The girls scooped up their sleeping bags. They ran for the house.

"Wait," Tasha called from the rear. "We have to save our tent."

Molly, Judy, and Lucy kept running for the house. Pegi and Maryellen and Lesley came back to help Tasha.

They yanked on the sheets. In two seconds the tent was apart. The girls pulled the sheets inside with them.

They all ran into the living room.

"Hey, what's going on?" Mr. Kearney said.

Tasha caught her breath. "Uh, we just decided to come inside."

Ty laughed. "They probably got scared," he said to Chad.

Chad nodded. "That's because they're girls."

Tasha glared at the two boys. "We were not scared. We—we were just getting cold."

Ty laughed even harder. "It must be ninety degrees outside! How can you be cold?"

"That's enough," Mr. Kearney said sternly. He got off the couch. "Come on, boys. Let's leave the girls alone."

With a groan, Ty and Chad got up.

"What a bunch of scaredy-cats," Ty mumbled.

As soon as they were alone, Tasha said, "They would have been scared too."

"Yeah," Lesley said.

"They think they're so brave," Judy said.

"Boys are such a pain," Molly grumbled.

"Especially my brother and his friend," Tasha said. "Now come on. Let's build a tent in here."

Lucy draped a sheet over a chair. "Now no monsters or ghosts can get us."

"Or a werewolf either," Pegi added.

Tasha laughed. "No matter how hungry he is."

The girls giggled. It was nice to feel safe inside.

Quickly, they put up a tent. Then they placed their sleeping bags inside it.

Tasha turned off the lights so it was really dark in the living room.

Finally they were settled inside the tent once again.

"Maybe we shouldn't tell any more scary stories," Tasha said.

"I like that idea," Lucy said with a shiver. "I've had enough scary stories to last me forever."

"Let's play truth, dare, double dare, promise, or repeat," Molly said eagerly.

"I'll go first," Judy said. "I want a double dare."

"I double dare you to call Timmy's house right now," Molly said.

Judy rolled her eyes. "That's not a double dare. That's easy."

"I'm not finished," Molly said with a grin. "You have to tell Ricky you have a crush on him."

Lucy squealed with delight and clapped her hands.

Judy groaned. "I can't do that," she exclaimed.

Molly laughed. "You have to. You said you wanted a double dare."

Tasha ran to get the portable phone and her phone book. She looked up Timmy's number and dialed it. Then she handed the phone to Judy.

Judy crossed her eyes at her friends, who crowded around. They all tried to listen at the earpiece.

"Hello?" Timmy answered.

"Hi," Judy said. "This is Judy."

"Judy who?" Timmy asked.

"Very funny," Judy said. "It's Judy Liu from school. Is Ricky there?"

"Ricky who?" Timmy asked with a snort of laughter.

Judy ground her teeth together. "Just let me talk to him."

"Ricky, oh, Rickyyyyy," Timmy called to his friend. "There's a girl who wants to talk to you."

Tasha and her friends laughed silently. This was a great double dare.

Ricky finally got on the phone. "Yeah?" he said.

"Hi, Ricky, this is Judy," Judy said in a rush. "I, uh, I, uh, I have a crush on you, bye!" Quickly she pushed the hang-up button. She fell back on the floor, laughing along with everyone else.

"That was great," Tasha said when she got her breath back. "Who wants to go next?"

Lucy suddenly clutched Tasha's hand. "What was that? I heard something!"

12
One, Two, Three, Boo!

Suddenly everyone was silent.

"I heard it too," Pegi whispered, pulling down the brim of her baseball cap.

"The monster is in the house!" Judy cried.

"But how did it get in?" Lesley asked.

Tasha bit her lip. "I think I left the porch door open!"

"Oh, noooo," Maryellen groaned.

"Maybe we can scare it away," Pegi suggested.

Tasha nodded. "If we all jump up at once and yell 'Boo!' the monster will run away."

"I'm too scared," Lucy said.

Tasha patted her friend's shoulder. "What choice do we have?"

"We have to do it," Pegi agreed.

All the girls nodded.

"On the count of three," Tasha instructed.

The girls crouched by the edges of the tent. They were ready to jump out and scare away the monster for good. Even Lucy was ready.

Tasha took a deep breath. "One . . . two . . . three—"

With a loud "BOO!" the girls jumped out of the tent.

But what they saw made them scream louder.

"It's a ghost!" yelled Maryellen.

A large, bulky ghost lumbered toward them.

Ty and Chad raced into the dark living room. When they saw the ghost they stopped short. "Ahhhh!" they screamed.

Suddenly, someone started laughing.

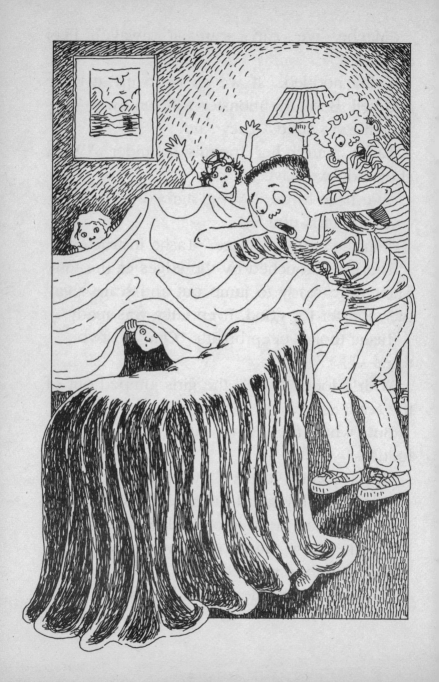

Everyone looked over at the boys. But they were still screaming. Their mouths were wide open. Their eyes bulged out of their heads.

Everyone looked around. Who was laughing?

Tasha!

Tasha laughed and snorted so hard, her sides ached.

She tripped over all the sheets and sleeping bags to get to the light switch. She turned on the lights.

Suddenly, the clumsy ghost wiggled at the back end. The sheet started to slip to one side. A loud "woof!" came from under the sheet.

"Hey, that isn't a ghost," Lucy said. She started to laugh.

"It's Daffy!" Tasha said.

The sheet came off the dog. Daffy jumped around the room, barking and wiggling her rear end.

Tasha scratched her uncle's dog behind the ears. She noticed some red sauce in Daffy's fur. "Daffy must have eaten the pizzas, too."

Ty and Chad's mouths still hung open.

"What's the matter, boys?" Tasha teased. "Were you afraid of a little old ghost?"

The boys closed their mouths with a snap.

"We were not afraid," Ty said. "We just came in to see what you were screaming about."

Tasha crossed her arms. "You sure looked scared. And you sounded scared, too."

"What do you expect from boys?" Pegi asked.

All the girls laughed.

"Now we can tell scary stories again," Mary-ellen said.

"Do you want to stay and listen?" Tasha asked her brother. "If you don't think you'll get too scared, that is."

The boys grinned. "We had better stay in case you girls get scared."

Everyone laughed.

Tasha looked around at her friends. She didn't even mind that Ty and Chad were part of her party.

Eight is great, she said to herself. And this has been the best sleepover party ever!

HOW TO HAVE A
SLEEPOVER PARTY

Sleepover parties are fun to have any time of year, and for any reason. Birthdays are a great reason, of course, but you and your friends can find lots of other things to celebrate with a sleepover party.

Sleepover Snacks

Food is very important at a sleepover party. Tasha thought of a great snack and drink to serve early on at the party. This also makes a yummy midnight snack (just in case you stay up that late!).

FUNTASTIC FIZZLE. First, fill tall glasses with ice. Then fill each glass halfway with a favorite kind of juice. Purple grape juice or red berry juice works really well for this drink. Fill up the glasses the rest of the way with lemon-lime soda—the fizzier the better! Make sure to stop pouring before the fizz overflows.

Next, you can decorate each glass with a fancy straw and a toothpick with fruit on it. Pineapple chunks, grapes, and cherries look fancy and taste yummy.

Everyone at Tasha's party loved the GOOD GOLLY GOBS. And they're so easy to make! First, mix together in a bowl 1 cup each of the following snack foods: nuts (peanuts work great); any kind of unsweetened cereal (Chex or Corn Flakes are tasty); small bits of pretzels; mini marshmallows; and anything else you can think of that's small and munchy and crunchy (like caramel popcorn or M & M's).

Now ask an adult to help you melt ¾ of a cup of chocolate chips. It's easiest to ask an adult to show you how to melt chocolate in a double boiler. If you don't have one at home, you and an adult can try it this way. Fill a large, deep, flat cast-iron skillet or frying pan halfway up with water, place on a stove burner, and bring the water to a boil. When the water begins to boil, turn off the stove and remove the pan from the burner. Place the chocolate chips in a small pot, and place the pot in the pan of hot water. Stir the chocolate constantly until it is completely melted. Be careful not to let any of the water splash onto the chocolate. Finally, pour the melted chocolate over your snack mixture and stir it around in the bowl with a big spoon. Let it sit for a couple of hours, and as the chocolate cools, it will clump the bits of pretzel together with the cereal and nuts, giving you good golly gobs to eat.

Of course, after your friends are finished snacking, they'll be hungry for dinner. Tasha and her friends had a lot of fun creating their own PIZZAS. They would have had fun eating them too, if Daffy hadn't gotten to them first. So be careful to leave your pizzas in a safe place while they cool!

Pizzas are easy to make and an all-time sleepover party favorite. Make sure you buy pizza dough ahead of time at the supermarket. When you're ready to create your pizza, sprinkle flour on the surface you will be working on and spread it all around. Using a rolling pin, roll out the pizza dough until it's big enough to fit on a round pizza pan or cookie sheet. Now, spread on the tomato sauce and sprinkle mozzarella cheese on top. You can also prepare lots of different toppings, such as pepperoni, mushrooms, olives, onions, pineapple, and ham. What are some of your favorite pizza toppings? Ask an adult to follow the pizza dough-baking directions. Before you know it, you'll be munching on homemade pizza.

When you're finished with your pizzas, you'll be ready for dessert. SUNDAES are fun and easy to make. And who doesn't like ice cream? Let your friends top off their ice cream with nuts, chocolate bits, chopped-up candy bars, bananas, caramel sauce, and whipped cream.

In the morning, Tasha served INITIAL PAN-CAKES for breakfast. To make this creative meal with your friends, simply buy pancake mix ahead of time. Then follow the directions on the package to make the pancake batter. Ask an adult to heat a pan on the stove and to help you pour the batter into the pan in the shapes of different letters. Make a different letter for each friend. Cook the letters on both sides until they're golden brown. Tasha ate a "T" for breakfast. Lucy ate an "L." Before your friends eat their pancakes, they can decorate them with syrup, jam, sugar, and cinnamon mix, or even chocolate chips! What a yummy breakfast.

Party Games

Food wasn't the only fun attraction at Tasha's sleepover party. Her friends also had fun playing games and doing different activities.

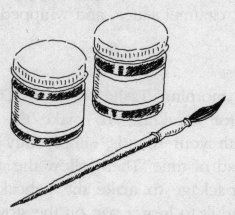

Tasha likes to draw and paint, so FACE PAINTING was a perfect thing to do at her party. Maybe you would like to do it, too. First you'll need to buy acrylic, water-based paints at your local craft store. You can even ask the clerk if there are special face paints. You'll also need a couple of small paintbrushes.

When you're painting your friends' cheeks, you don't need to be fancy. A simple sun or star or colorful design is all you need to impress your friends.

Another activity Tasha and her friends enjoyed was TRUTH OR DARE. They also added double dare, promise, and repeat. Take turns challenging each other. If a person picks *truth*, she has to answer a personal question truthfully. *Dare* and *Double dare* mean the person has to do something daring, like when Judy had to call Ricky. A dare could also be to flap like a chicken or snort like a hog. Just don't ask your friends to do anything dangerous or something you wouldn't do.

If someone picks *promise*, she has to promise to tell or do what is asked of her. And if she picks *repeat*, she has to repeat whatever someone tells her to repeat, like "I love Timmy and think his stupid jokes are really the funniest things in the world."

LIGHT AS A FEATHER, STIFF AS A BOARD is a fun and scary game to play at a sleepover party. Have one person lie down and pretend to be the "victim." Everyone else forms a tight circle around her. Each person puts two fingers under the "victim."

Then, one person tells a really scary story about how the "victim" was "scared to death." At the end of the story, the storyteller says, "the 'victim' is as light as a feather and as stiff as a board. And when I count to three, we will lift the 'victim' into the air with just our fingers. One. Two. Three." Then everyone lifts. If the story was scary enough, you'll be able to lift the "victim" a foot off the ground with no problem!

Happy Endings

Finally, a party isn't a party without a party favor. A LOLLIPOP BOUQUET is as much fun to make as it is to receive. First, buy an assortment of lollipops and ribbon. Five to ten lollipops for each bouquet should be plenty.

Gather the lollipops for the first bouquet together and secure them with a rubber band. Tie some ribbon in a bow around the rubber band so that the rubber band is hidden. To make your bouquet even more special, you can tie a toy, a hair barrette, or a piece of costume jewelry onto the ribbon with a piece of yarn or string. You can also make miniature name tags for each bouquet. Your friends will be sweet on these colorful party favors, and sweet on you for being so thoughtful!

Tasha and her friends had a super time at her sleepover. And you will too!

Look for more LET'S HAVE A PARTY

Have Your Own Party! Fun Tips in Every Book

#1 SCHOOL'S OUT!
78925-6/$3.99 US/$4.99 Can

#2 SPLASH!
78922-1/$3.99 US/$4.99 Can

#3 SLEEPOVER
78924-8/$3.99 US/$4.99 Can

#4 SURPRISE!
78921-3/$3.99 US/$4.99 Can

And coming soon
#5 BOO WHO?
79256-7/$3.99 US/$4.99 Can

#6 THANKSGIVING FIESTA
79257-5/$3.99 US/$4.99 Can

#7 SECRET SANTA
79258-3/$3.99 US/$4.99 Can